Maisie Middleton at the Wedding

Nita Sowter

CARNIVAL

It was a hot afternoon
at Maisie Middleton's house.
Maisie was in her secret place
at the bottom of the garden.

"Maisie, Maisie!" called Mummy.
"Aunt Rosy's here and she has
some good news. Come inside."

Maisie ran in quickly
because she liked her aunt.
"Hello, Maisie," said Aunt Rosy.
"I've got something very special
to tell you. I'm getting married
and I want you to be my bridesmaid."
There was a long silence.
"Oh," said Maisie.

Maisie tried to forget all about
being a bridesmaid, and spent
a lot of time in her secret place.

"I don't want to be a soppy bridesmaid
and wear a silly, scratchy, frilly,
beastly dress," Maisie told the animals.

Then one day Mummy called her.
"Maisie, Maisie. Come here, please.
It's time to try on your dress."

"I'm doing things,"
said Maisie.
But Mummy kept
on calling and
calling.
"Maisie Middleton,
COME HERE."

Maisie went slowly
into the house.

Mummy put the
dress on Maisie.
"Ow," said Maisie.
"It ITCHES and
TICKLES," and
she stomped and
wriggled.
"Maisie Middleton,
stand still," said
Mummy.
"OUCH, OUCH,
OUCH," said
Maisie.

The next afternoon George came to tea.
"I'm going to be a pageboy at the wedding,"
he said.
"It'll be really good. After the church bit,
you sit at a big table and eat lots of food.
All the grown-ups smile and smile, and
they don't tell you off if you eat more puddings."

"Hmmm," said Maisie.

The wedding day arrived.
"We'll go upstairs and get
ready now," said Mummy.
"I'm not going to like this,"
said Maisie.

But the dress did look very pretty and it felt soft, and not scratchy at all. Maisie spun round and round – wheeeee. Perhaps it won't be so awful after all, thought Maisie, as she went downstairs. "Look at Maisie," said Mummy. "Lovely," said everybody.

Eventually Aunt Rosy was ready.
"Ooooh – look!" whispered Maisie to George.
"Just like a Fairy Godmother."
"Come on, we're late," said Daddy.
"There's a wedding to get to."

"RUN," said Maisie.

"... and I pronounce you man and wife," the vicar said. The organ played dum, dum, de dum.

The bride and groom kissed
and walked out into the afternoon sunshine.

"Hurrah, hurrah," everyone said.
"Line up here," said the photographer.
Click, click, click, click. "Thank you."

Now it was time for the grand wedding feast.
Maisie and George stared at all the wonderful
food laid out on the tables.

"Ooh, look at those puddings,"
sighed Maisie.

Maisie and George were very hungry
after all the church business.

"Here's a toast to the Happy Couple,
and here's a toast to Maisie and George.
Now it's time to cut the cake," said Daddy.

Then the band struck up and the dancing began.
Round and round they whirled,
faster and faster.
Suddenly Maisie felt a bit tired,
so she and George found a nice quiet place
to sit down and rest.

It was very late.
The moon shone through the window
as Mummy snuggled Maisie down in bed.
Maisie Middleton smiled as she slept,
dreaming of weddings, dancing and puddings.

The next day Maisie told all
the animals about it.
Maisie and George became good friends,
and they played weddings with the animals
in the garden.

And when the wedding photographs came,
Maisie and George looked at them for a very,
very long time.